Across the Sea from Galway

Across the Sea from Galway

written and illustrated by Leonard Everett Fisher

FOUR WINDS PRESS   NEW YORK

Library of congress cataloging in publication data

Fisher, Leonard Everett.
   Across the sea from Galway.

   Summary: In 1849, following the potato famine, an Irish boy and
his brother and sister are sent by their parents on an ill-fated journey
to Boston.
   [1. Irish in the United States—Fiction. 2. Ireland—Famines—
Fiction] I. Title.
   PZ7.F533Ac   [Fic]   75–9513
   ISBN 0–590–07345–1

———•◆•———

Published by Four Winds Press
A Division of Scholastic Magazines, Inc., New York, N.Y.
Copyright © 1975 by Leonard Everett Fisher
All rights reserved
Printed in the United States of America
Library of Congress Catalog Card Number: 75–9513
1 2 3 4 5   79 78 77 76 75

To Malcolm Reiss

Also written and illustrated by Leonard Everett Fisher

Picture Books
PUMPERS, BOILERS, HOOKS AND LADDERS
PUSHERS, SPADS, JENNIES AND JETS
A HEAD FULL OF HATS

Nonfiction
THE COLONIAL AMERICANS (18 VOLUMES)
  GLASSMAKERS, SILVERSMITHS, PAPERMAKERS,
  PRINTERS, WIGMAKERS, HATTERS, SHOEMAKERS,
  TANNERS, POTTERS, LIMNERS, SHIPBUILDERS,
  HOMEMAKERS, CABINETMAKERS, ARCHITECTS,
  WEAVERS, PEDDLERS, SCHOOLMASTERS, DOCTORS
TWO IF BY SEA
PICTURE BOOK OF REVOLUTIONARY WAR HEROES
THE ART EXPERIENCE: OIL PAINTING 15TH-19TH CENTURY

Fiction
THE DEATH OF EVENING STAR
THE WARLOCK OF WESTFALL
SWEENEY'S GHOST

Across the Sea from Galway

Part One

Cohasset

My gentle harp,
Once more I waken
The sweetness of thy slumb'ring strain,
In tears
Our last farewell was taken,
And now in tears
We meet again.

Yet even then,
While peace was singing
Her halcyon song o'er land and sea,
Though joy and hope
To others bringing,
She only brought
New tears to thee.

from *My Gentle Harp* by Thomas Moore

1

Several hundred people stood silent and motionless on the rock-strewn Cohasset beach at Pleasant Cove. Several hundred more would join them before this Tuesday, October 9, 1849, would pass into the silo of memory.

"Death," proclaimed a Boston news poster. "One hundred forty-five lives lost at Cohasset."

The funeral would be this afternoon.

From a distance, the large congregation and scattered boulders looked like a mile-long row of broken pillars; the irregular remnant of some forgotten ruin or civilization, breaching the sands that failed to bury it all. A closer view revealed a stricken crowd, dark and foreboding, awaiting the final verdict of the New England sea—Life or Death—for mother, father, sister, or brother; sons and daughters; cousins and strangers.

It was as if an anxious multitude had risen through the sand, summoned to account by heavenly trumpets or to bear witness to another's eternal sentence. This was Judgment Day. And, although a pale sun hung like a wayfarer's beacon in the gray morning sky for the first time in a week, it brightened nothing, soothed no one.

Sunday's storm was Tuesday's grief. The appearance of the sun made little difference to the despair of those on the Cohasset beach who searched the watery grave of the brig **St. John,** recently out of Galway, Ireland. The vessel, once briefly crowded with hopeful immigrants to the New World, now lay smashed beyond help and hope on Grampus Rock, one mile from the Massachusetts shore, one mile from deliverance.

The heaving sea, still caught by the northeaster's diminishing winds, drove its terror at the beachside congregation with those relentless, everlasting rhythms that seamen challenge and voyagers fear. It hissed and foamed at their feet. It soaked the shoes and clothing of those who dared the sea to take them too. The wild water receded. But it came back. Again and again and again. It lashed at the rocks and floating debris. It rolled over broken spars, tangled line, chunks of deck, timber, braces, and every bit of mangled flotsam and seaweed a gale-struck ship-wreck could yield—including the lives and dreams of many on board—145 Irish pilgrims—men, women and children. Few survived.

Every so often, someone, some group, would rustle and leave the silent, watchful line, beckoned to another part of the beach by a solicitous, weary official of the Massachusetts Humane Society. A sheet would be lifted; a coffin's contents inspected. A terrible sob would float on the wind and quickly vanish. A vigil had ended.

"Listen, Francie," an old woman whispered to her companion. "Do you hear that?"

"Aye, Katie, I hear it. The poor soul. A relative no doubt. And from what county do you suppose?"

"Relative, Francie? County? It's the shriek I'm mindful of. The shriek. Have you no ear? It's Banshee's wail, Francie—all the way from Erin. Saints preserve us all!"

"Aye, Katie, now that you mention it. It's her all right. It's the Banshee. Listen! There it goes again. I know that screech well. I've heard her many times before in the old country."

"And you'll hear it a few times more, Francie; a few times more—in the new country."

[5]

"Glory Be and Saints preserve us, Katie. Will you be staying for the funeral?"

"Aye, Francie. We are them and they are us. And we'll be planting a bit of Ireland in this stony ground. I'll be there to pray that the ground turns green with shamrock lest we forget who it is that's in that ground."

While the two women busied themselves with more observations and chatter, the atmospheric violence had quit. The howling winds had finally blown themselves into harmless offshore breezes. The restless sea had suddenly flattened as if spent by its destructive fit. There were those on the beach who convinced themselves that a great hand had pressed the mad sea down for the sake of the living. Whatever, all that remained of the turbulence of the past three or four days was a vast silence that seemed to have the mark of eternity on it—or so it felt for the moment.

Clearly visible, and seemingly within arm's reach, was a piece of the **St. John's** bow. Jutting out of the water and thrusting skyward, the lifeless, splintered timbers were rammed hard against Grampus Rock—a temporary monument to her own disaster. Soon the sea would claim those timbers and cover them over. Only Grampus Rock would survive and be reckoned with again.

A year later, a lighthouse would be built nearby to warn passing ships of the Minots and Cohasset Ledges—those shallow, rocky depths that tore apart the **St. John** and destroyed her cargo of Irish immigrants.

But on Sunday, October 7, 1849, there was no lighthouse. There was no warning.

[7]

2

Cohasset, that place on the Massachusetts coastal lowland where the Boston-bound **St. John** met her end, was, for the most part, a sleepy seaside resort village. There, while overheated Bostonians refreshed themselves on the soft summer sands, the enterprising villagers dragged up from the bottom an abundance of kelp, rockweed, and Irish moss for profit. Much of this seaweed, once cured, would find its way to American salads, soaps, and chemicals. And there was no calamity great enough to keep some gatherers from their perpetual toil.

While the Almighty harvested 145 unfortunate victims from the wreck of the brig, a few villagers walked behind their plodding wagon teams in another cove, nearby, harvesting the weeds flung ashore by the fury of the storm. And the tragedy of the **St. John** came and went and came again like the tide, before their very eyes. She was not the first, nor would she be the last to come to nothing on Grampus Rock. Such was the hard reality of New England rooted in an earlier day. Death, however distant, however near, always certain, was to be endured, not waited upon. Work went on. And work—in the Puritan realm —was the tax levied by God upon the backs of mortal men in return for His favors. Namely, survival.

Cohasset is about fifteen straight miles below the heart of Boston and, perhaps, twenty miles above Plymouth. But the town's presence on Massachusetts Bay, together with the Irish disaster on Grampus Rock, is firmly linked to America's dim primeval past and to the Puritans who settled the place in 1647. For here, to Cohasset, in the light of that past, came another band of seekers—not English Protestants, but Irish Catholics—pilgrims all. They came across the sea from Galway only to be victimized by a storm and a rock—only to have so many of **their** number wrenched from the promise of this New World without having touched the land they clearly saw.

Historically, and in that dim past, a small band of Indians called the site Conohasset. It was their village first. These Indians—in all probability, the Cutshamakins—belonged to the Massachuset tribe. And the Massachusets were part of the great Algonquian nation, a conglomeration of tribes—Wampanoag, Pennacook, Nauset, Mohican, among others—that spoke the same language.

When, in 1614, Captain John Smith came ashore at Conohasset on a mapping expedition, there were about three thousand Massachusets Indians scattered throughout the area which bore their name. Within twenty years there would not be five hundred of them. And by the time Conohasset was colonized by the English there were still fewer. In fact, there were hardly any to speak of. Tribal wars had taken their toll. Disease did the rest. Two hundred years later, none stood on the beach to mourn the fate of the brig, **St. John.**

In any event, Conohasset became Cohasset. And on the eve of the American Revolution, in the year of the Boston Massacre —1770—Cohasset was incorporated a town of the Massachusetts Bay Colony.

Over the next seventy-five years, the people of Cohasset fished, farmed, gathered their seaweed, and kept an eye on the constant movement of ships that crossed their horizon. How much of this traffic was doomed to break apart on the rocky undersea ledges that made up Cohasset's watery environment will never be known. Yet enough marine disasters occurred there to encourage the Humane Society of Massachusetts to station lifeboats manned by volunteers on those beaches.

And so it was that the good men of Cohasset, crusty with sea salt, whipped by the ocean winds, and heirs to the Puritan hardiness of their forbears, formed the crews for the first lifeboat service in America. All this not long before the loss of the **St. John.**

While some of their townsmen hauled away their Irish moss and kelp, a few heroic sailors launched those boats in a valiant effort to beat the gale and reach the screaming victims trapped aboard the brig on Grampus Rock.

So much for Cohasset.

3

The large beefy man knelt beside the blanketed pyramid and peered inside at a small boy seated on a stool.

"You must be very warm by now, young fellow. That's a fairly hot fire at your back, you know."

The boy made no reply.

The man rose. He picked up a heavy split log about two feet long and heaved it into the fire. He brushed his hands clean of some splinters and dirt and came back to the boy.

"Would you like to tell me your name, lad? You do have a name, don't you? We want to help."

"Patrick, sir." It was a quiet, listless response.

"Patrick? Patrick what? Do you have another?"

The fire snapped and sparked at the boy's back. He leaned forward slightly—not much.

"Easy, Timothy. Perhaps you'd best leave him be for now. He'll come round soon enough."

Abigail Murphy, as skinny and boney a woman as her husband, Tim Murphy, was large and muscular, stepped out of the gloomy recess at the far end of the room. She gently pulled her husband a few steps away from the figure inside the blanket.

"Maybe he'll come around, Abigail. Maybe not. Maybe never. There's a hurt inside him. He could not have been alone on that brig. He must have—or maybe had—a family."

"All that might very well be so, Timothy. All in good time. We ought not press the lad. Right now I think he's about to recover somewhat, eh? What name did he give?"

"Patrick."

"Well now, that's a start. Let us not be forgetting that he has had a terrible experience. The Lord was merciful. How this boy remained alive, unbruised, pinned by all that timber we'll never know."

"An Irish miracle, Mrs. Murphy."

"The Lord's miracle, Mr. Murphy. And what do you know about **Irish** miracles, granting there are such things. You've never even been to Ireland—only to Boston. Besides, you're forever boasting how your father was born the day **his** father took a British bullet on Bunker Hill while you yourself came squalling into this world on the Fourth of July—in Boston! I've been listening to your nonsense every day for twenty-five years. I suppose I'll just have to go on listening to it."

"I'll tell you what I know about Irish miracles, my good wife."

"Nothing," replied Abigail quickly. "But you go right on while I heat up this clam broth for the boy."

"My grandfather was Timothy Murphy. My father was Timothy Murphy. I am Timothy Murphy. Our seed was sown in County Mayo long before St. Patrick himself came to that green land. But we all saw the light of day in America. Born in Boston I tell you. And that, Mrs. Murphy, is an Irish miracle!"

"No, my good husband. That is a Yankee miracle. The Lord saw to that!" Abigail Murphy, whose ancestry was solid English Puritan, smiled sweetly at Tim and stirred the steamy broth.

"Why don't you go back down to the beach," she continued. "You'll be more help there than you are here. I'll tend to our Patrick."

Timothy Murphy turned and stalked out of the one room house that had been his and Abigail's childless cottage for more years than they wished to remember. The house was set on a sandy knoll about five hundred yards from the beach. Tim scrambled over the sand and rocks and dry brush. A few minutes later he had disappeared from view, still making his way to the growing, silent throng on the beach.

Abigail hooked the fireplace crane with a long iron rod and pulled it away from the flames. The kettle of steaming clam broth that hung there swayed back and forth for a moment or two. Abigail let it come to rest before she dipped a ladle into it and sipped.

"Good and hot!" she exclaimed, sucking in air as if to keep the tip of her tongue from blistering. "Just right for a cold, hungry lad. What say you, Patrick?"

Patrick was neither cold nor very hungry. If he felt anything at all it was the roasting fire at his back. More to the point, he was numb with confusion. The fate of his younger sister and older brother, Maureen and Sean, washed in and out of his mind like the rolling sea from which he was delivered.

Patrick, Maureen, and Sean were only three of five children belonging to Liam and Kathleen Donovan. A set of twins— girls, Mary and Margaret—remained behind with their mother and father. Liam and Kathleen Donovan could only scrape up enough money to send their three eldest children to America. They and the twins would have to wait and pray that it would not be a long separation.

Kathleen's bachelor brother, Brendan O'Sullivan, a Boston dockworker, had some idea that the family was coming. But when, to what port, how many of them—he could not be sure. Liam had written one short letter to him some months ago:

Dear Brendan,

May 28, 1849

Greetings. We hope this finds you in good spirits. We are going to Galway. We seek passage to America. There is much hunger here. Much unhappiness. No opportunities. We are none of us anxious to leave Erin. We must. We ask no favors of you—none—but to see a family face in America. I shall write again with arrangements. May the Saints protect you. May the Saints protect us.

In Faith and Hope, Yours
Liam Donovan

The blanketed form stirred. The aroma of the steamy clam broth had jarred the numb reverie of the boy inside the woolly folds. Abigail caught the slight shiver that passed through

[14]

Patrick Donovan. The blanket slipped back a little revealing some wild tufts of hair as red as the blaze in the fireplace. It was as if the shades of night were slowly yielding to the light of the rising sun.

Patrick made no move to pull the blanket back up around him. It fell away a few more inches, enough to uncover his head. Abigail moved toward him. Gently, she lifted away the warm covering. Patrick let her do it without protest. Silently, neatly, she folded it and placed it in a heavy wood chest.

Patrick sat there, on the stool, still unmoving. In the flickering lights and darks of the snapping fire, he appeared much thinner, much knobbier and a good deal smaller than he actually was. Tim Murphy's baggy clothes did not help Patrick's appearance either. Temporarily engulfed by Tim's enormous homespun yardage—his own patchy clothing shredded by the angry sea—Patrick was pitifully lost in the hollow strangeness that served only to exaggerate the already empty space of his lonely nightmare.

"Here lad, try this," said Abigail. She all but thrust the bowl of hot broth into his hands. "It will do you some good, you'll see."

Patrick gripped the scalding bowl, unmindful of its heat and seemingly unmindful of its very presence in his hands. Abigail did not press him further. She just stood to one side and waited. A half minute later, Patrick lifted the bowl to his lips and drained it in one long gulp.

"Another?"

"Yes, ma'am."

"Ah! That's a good lad. You have another. And we'll talk some. That is if you have a mind to. Mr. Murphy will be back soon with good news, I am sure, and then we'll all be having something more substantial to eat. You can't go on drinking clam broth forever."

"Yes, ma'am."

Patrick drained the second bowl as he had done the first—in one long gulp.

"Now lad, would you do a poor old lady a favor? Would you tell me your name?"

"Patrick, ma'am."

"I know that. Tim Murphy knows that. What we'd like to know is your family name, lad. How can we help you find your relatives without a family name? You do have relatives, I trust?"

"Yes ma'am."

"And their name?"

"Donovan, ma'am."

"Then you are Patrick Donovan?"

"Patrick Michael Donovan, ma'am."

"Good lad. And what of the rest of the Donovans, Patrick? Would you like to tell me about them? It would be of help to you if you did."

"There's not much to tell, ma'am. My mother, father, and the baby girls—they're twins—are still in Ireland. There was not enough money for all of us to make the passage together. Maureen and Sean—my sister and brother—were on the brig with me. They are dead, ma'am. I saw them."

There was not a tear in Patrick's eyes nor in his voice. Stony, expressionless, he was too numb to accept the horror that came to him, and to his sister and brother, in the waters of Cohasset, Massachusetts, three thousand miles from the only home they had ever known.

Patrick Michael Donovan droned on. He seemed to need no further urging from Abigail Murphy.

"The brig hit something. All at once it came apart. We were down below in the forward part—Maureen, Sean, and me—when it happened. Suddenly, we were in the water, together. I do not know how we got there. It was misty and rough. Cold, too. I held on to some wreckage. Sean had one arm around the same timbers and another around Maureen. A great wave rose above us. It smashed us. After it passed, I found myself on some other timbers. My legs were caught by something. I could not free them. There were people all around now, screaming and drowning. A small boat came alongside. I could almost touch it. It was full of people. That's when I saw them—Maureen and Sean. They were in the boat. But then the boat filled with water. It sank out of sight. So did everyone in it. That's all I remember except waking up in this house. Is this America, ma'am?"

"Yes, Patrick. This is America. And lucky you are to be here."

Abigail did not know what else to say. She was too stunned beyond any real comforting words. Patrick's tragic tale and the immensity of the entire disaster had overtaken her.

Patrick broke the momentary silence. "I have an uncle, ma'am. His name is O'Sullivan—Brendan O'Sullivan. He lives in Boston. I think my father wrote to him about our coming. Is Boston far away?"

"No. Do you know your uncle well?"

"No, ma'am. He is my mother's brother. I never saw him."

Before Abigail could pursue this, Tim Murphy came through the door. Abigail motioned for him to step outside with her. Tim followed. She told her husband all that Patrick had related during the past few minutes.

"He has an uncle in Boston, Timothy. We could try to find him. He knew the Donovans were coming over. He may very well be down at the beach right now. The only trouble is Patrick does not know him on sight."

"No matter," replied Timothy. There are so many down there now we could never find him in time."

"In time for what?"

"There is to be a funeral for all of the victims this afternoon. We are trying to have identified as many of the victims as is possible before they are buried. If the lad's sister and brother are laid out there on the beach, the only one who could know who they are—or were—is the lad himself. I think we had best get Patrick Michael Donovan down there."

"Timothy Murphy! You cannot put him through such agony. Hasn't young Patrick been through enough as it is? This is unnecessary I tell you!"

"You are not his mother, Abigail. You are not his Guardian Angel either. He is a boy. He will soon be a man. The shock he suffers now, Abigail, and the shock he might suffer on that beach will be nothing compared to the doubt that will fester in him throughout his life if he can never be certain that some of the bones in that grave belong to him. He has a duty to himself and his kin. I may have never been to Ireland, but just the same, you do not know the Irish as I do. They are easily given over to melancholy. If you want to make a hopeless drunkard out of the lad—and it will surely come to pass—then you keep him from going down to the beach to look at the truth—if it is there."

Abigail remained silent.

"It may very well be," Tim continued, "that the lad was imagining things; that his sister and brother are alive and looking for him. If that is so, then that's another good reason to get him down there."

Timothy Murphy, weary and edgy from the excesses of death that had come ashore at Cohasset, put his arm around his wife and sniffed the air. "And don't give me any of your smart English sass on the subject. I smell clam broth. If it's still hot I'll have some. I need a little of the life it will pump through my veins.

"Come, Abigail. Let us go back inside. We cannot leave that young Patrick Michael Donovan in there alone. He is going to need all the strength we can give him."

4

The solemn procession came up from the beach. Slowly, hundreds of marchers shuffled their way toward the Cohasset Common and the graveyard. There, they were awaited by a number of town officials, several area ministers, and several Catholic priests from Boston including young Father Thomas J. Walsh whose recently ordained brother, Kevin, was among those lost in the disaster.

Leading the procession, and all alone, was the hatless captain of the **St. John.** His walk was straight and steady. Under his left arm he carried the proud flag that had fluttered from the top

foremast when the **St. John** caught an easterly wind and sailed out of Galway Bay for Boston—Ireland's ancient green banner emblazoned with a gold harp. The flag had washed up intact. It was quickly rescued by some of the crowd and stretched out to dry with rocks placed at all four corners to keep it from flying away.

True to the tradition of the sea, the captain did everything he could for his hapless passengers and stricken vessel. But, however well intended, it wasn't very much. There was little time for heroics. The **St. John** began to break up beneath his feet almost immediately upon being grounded. As the pieces of the ship began to settle into the water, the captain raced for the quarter deck to have a better look at his situation. There, he was promptly knocked off the ship by a wildly swinging spar. Unhurt, he was heaved up onto the beach by the boiling sea about fifteen or twenty minutes later. Half out of his mind with exhaustion and anguish, but still determined to do something, he flung himself back into the sea in a vain attempt to return to the ship. But the sea hurled him back onto the beach. And there he lay, helpless and sobbing, no longer the master, his power sucked from him by the insatiable sea.

Walking a few yards behind the **St. John**'s captain were a half dozen members of her crew—all that remained alive and unscathed. They were followed by a handful of survivors— those who could walk. Patrick was not among them. He had gone down to the beach with the Murphys after some coaxing. But there he remained, refusing to budge, sitting amidst the wreckage, staring at the rippling sea. The Cohasset beach held no truth for him one way or another. Maureen and Sean had vanished. It was too unreal. This great adventure, this great

[21]

voyage would never be completed now. He was alone in the New World—alone among strangers. Not even an image of Uncle Brendan crossed his mind. How could it? Brendan O'Sullivan was a name. Nothing more. Abigail Murphy sat nearby.

Next in the procession, in single file, were a number of horse-drawn wagons. One of the drivers was Timothy Murphy. Each wagon carried some of the roughly boxed remains of the thirty or thirty-five victims who were recovered from the sea. On happier, ordinary days, the wagons were filled with kelp, rock weed, and Irish moss. Tomorrow, Wednesday, it would rain torrents. Thursday would be an ordinary day. Of the more than one hundred others lost, a few more would be found. Maureen and Sean Donovan, late of Galway, once removed from Ballingarry, County Tipperary, Ireland, would not be among them. The New England sea would be their eternity.

Finally, there was the great line of mourners. In twos and threes, singly and in clusters, they silently followed the wagons. So many people fell into the line of march there were hardly any spectators.

By four o'clock in the afternoon it was all over.

The Lord had given. The Lord had taken.

The captain of the **St. John,** together with some of his crewmen unfolded the green banner of old Erin emblazoned with the gold harp. They spread it out over the single massive grave now filled in with the soil of Cohasset. Again the four corners were held fast by some rocks lest that flag of Irish presence flutter away.

"There, Francie," said the old woman who, true to her word, returned for the funeral. "There, that does it. That blessed ground is Ireland now."

"Aye, Katie," added her companion. "That it is! And how green it is too. The poor souls never did leave the old sod, did they?"

Part Two

Ballingarry

The minstrel boy to the war is gone,
In the ranks of death you'll find him;
His father's sword he has girded on,
And his wild harp slung behind him.
"Land of Song!" said the warrior bard,
"Though all the world betrays thee,
One sword, at least, thy rights shall guard,
One faithful harp shall praise thee."

The minstrel fell, but the foeman's chain
Could not bring that proud soul under.
The harp he loved ne'er spoke again,
For he tore its chords asunder;
And said, "No chain shall sully thee,
Thou soul of love and bravery;
Thy songs were made for the pure and free,
They shall never sound in slavery."

from *The Minstrel Boy* by Thomas Moore

5

By his own reckoning, Liam Donovan sprang full grown from the soil of County Clare.

"I am Ireland," he would cry out. "My mother was the sweet dirt of Kilfenora; my father—a potato."

In a way, Liam Donovan was Ireland; or at least, everyman's idea of the Irish spirit. For what other being in this world—save an Irishman—could painfully describe himself to be a bastard child and at the same time triumphantly transform the sin of his parentage into the awesome, God-like power of a whole land and its people—and do this so poetically, so musically; with such humor and simplicity?

"I am Ireland. My mother was the sweet dirt of Kilfenora; my father—a potato."

The plain fact is that Liam Donovan's mother was a dairymaid. His father was a wandering minstrel. And he, Liam, was the product of their unwed union. In the clannish, hidebound familial codes of Catholic Ireland, this was an unacceptable abomination. Worse still, to all intents and purposes, not only was Liam Donovan a bastard child, he was an orphan child— a redheaded, week-old infant left behind by his unmarried lusting parents, who took to the high road and were never seen again. Liam Donovan was abandoned for others to feed. And that was an offense to the impoverished peasantry who could not feed themselves too well.

"This is Liam Donovan," said his wayward mother one night to a surprised Kilfenora farmwife. "He's yours." With that she set young Liam down at the woman's feet and fled into the gloom.

Liam grew up haunted by his misbegotten beginnings. He knew all about himself. The Harrigans—Paddy, Mollie, and their seven children, the family that took him in—never let him forget who and what he was. They worked him more than they fed him. It was as if they were determined to have one small boy make the few boggy acres prosper. But the land yielded little, overrun as it was by **the little people**— elves, fairies and leprechauns. The Harrigans were convinced of that!

"Do you believe in the little people, Liam Donovan?" they always asked.

"No, I don't believe in the little people," he always replied. "But don't go out into those fields at night without a moon or they'll knock you down."

Such was the mind and impishness of Liam Donovan. But in the end, lean and hard though still a boy, Liam crossed the Harrigan fields one moonless, drizzly night. No one knocked him down. He never looked back. He never came back—not to stand on those particular acres, anyway. Instead, he became a roving beggar-minstrel; a singer of songs like his unknown father before him.

For the next ten years, Liam Donovan wandered over the face of Ireland. There was not a county in the entire land, not a corner of Ireland that he did not tramp over, singing for his bed, bread, and coin: from County Kerry in the southwest to County Wexford in the southeast; to Counties Mayo, Donegal, Monaghan, and Louth in the north. He crisscrossed them all: Counties Sligo, Roscommon, Offaly, Kilkenny, Cork, Kildare, Dublin, and more.

Wherever he spread his charm and imagination, small crowds would gather. When the music was done, the talk would turn to

their endless poverty; to the enslaving yoke of the British land-lord; to the British laws that kept them down; to freedom. And when all the words were spoken, someone would bellow, "Sing it, Liam. Sing it loud and clear, lad. Let them hear it in London Town." And Liam would sing:

"Oh, Paddy dear, and did ye hear the news that's goin'
    round?
The shamrock is by law forbid to grow on Irish ground.
No more Saint Patrick's Day we'll keep, his colors can't be
    seen,
For there's a cruel law ag'in the Wearin' o' the Green."

On and on he would sing. Sometimes Liam would sing all alone. And when he would finish, he'd try to move on. But the crowd would not let him budge. They would make him sing the **Wearin' o' the Green** all over again until he was too weary to continue. At times, and except for Liam's rising voice, the place would be so quiet that a field mouse could almost be heard streaking across the dirt floor. And during these special times, when the only voice was Liam's, the faces of his audience would harden with anger over their British masters. And their eyes would gleam with thoughts of a free Ireland; of free Irishmen; of plenty to eat and money to spend.

More often the crowd would join in with a rousing final chorus of the **Wearin' o' the Green**. Again someone would roar from the heart of the crowd. Only this time it would be, "Erinn go bragh. Ireland forever!" And the songfest would be over.

One bright spring morning, Liam Donovan walked into the village of Ballingarry, County Tipperary. He was on his way

[31]

west toward Limerick. There, at a tiny sod hut with a straw roof, he stopped for water. Liam never wandered again. He remained to sing for the friendly impoverished family who lived in the hut—Seamus O'Sullivan, a widower; his son, Brendan; and his pretty daughter, Kathleen. But the songs were for Kathleen. A year later they were married. Liam was twenty-five; Kathleen twenty. That was in 1832.

6

The O'Sullivans, father and son; and the Donovans, Kathleen and Liam, worked the land. But the land was not theirs. They owned not one square inch of it. It belonged to a wealthy English peer, their landlord, who did not even live on Irish soil. He preferred to remain on his English estates outside of London. Instead, he provided an overseer to manage his Irish affairs, collect his rents and taxes, and generally see to it that his tenant-farmers obeyed the system or be run off the land to nowhere.

Except for a small plot of ground upon which they grew potatoes and vegetables—mostly potatoes—whatever else they harvested belonged to the landlord. That was the rent they paid for the privilege of remaining alive on a diet of potatoes and vegetables, provided, of course, they raised a decent crop for themselves. The several hens that they owned produced a few eggs. But these were of little comfort. The eggs were sold from time to time to pay taxes that the landlord exacted from them whenever he thought it necessary. Every so often, the overseer would descend on them and simply take the eggs.

The rolling hills that surrounded the family were green and breathtaking. The lowlands they farmed were naturally damp and fertile. The lakes and rivers of the countryside sparkled like blue diamonds. But they, the O'Sullivans and the Donovans, were in rags, their feet bare, and their bodies slowly thinning from near starvation. None of this was new. It was an ageless affliction of the Irish people.

Liam Donovan sang less and less. Brendan O'Sullivan cursed more and more. His father, wracked by the pains of old age, brooded over his pointless life. Kathleen remained the most cheerful of the lot even after she became pregnant and took to her straw bed, too weak to stand.

Liam and Brendan spent long hours discussing and reviewing their plight.

"Why do we work so hard, Liam? Are we any better off for it? Do our lives improve because of it?"

"We work like animals," Liam replied, "so that we may live as animals. If we slacken we shall die. Do you want that, Brendan?"

"Holy Mother of God, Liam! I want to live! We all want to live! But not like this! We want improvement. That's what we want!"

"So it's improvement you want, Brendan."

"Aye, **improvement!**"

"Let me tell you about improvement. If we improve our situation; if we better our methods and increase our produce; if we own one more hen than we now have; our rents will rise, our taxes will rise and we shall be as we are now."

"Bah!"

"Bah! Is it? You were present the other day when poor Tom Finnegan and his whole family were flung from the land—and by the British infantry, no less—because they could pay neither the rent nor the tax. And why couldn't they pay? Because they improved the land and the produce from it and could no longer afford the increased tariffs they were made to swallow. The Finnegans weren't improved, now, were they?"

"Maybe there are other ways, Liam."

"What are you suggesting, Brendan? That we knock off the Lion's crown; that we tear out the Lion's heart; that we let the British Throne know that Finn McCool is the King of all Erin?"

"Aye. And why not, Liam. Why not war on the British. Look what the Yankees did!"

"I'll tell you why not, Brendan. Because now is not the time. The day will come. Of that you can be sure. But right now it would take a million Irishmen, each with a gun, to stand up to the likes of the British army. And who would be our general? Finn McCool? A ghost? And tell me, Brendan, where is your gun?"

"I don't have one."

"And neither do I. And neither did Tom Finnegan. All he had was a club. And neither does anyone else have a gun."

"Then we have to get guns!"

"Where?"

"In America, Liam. In America."

"Then you had better go to America and get them, Brendan."

"I will. But not until after I'm an uncle."

Other than the fact that Brendan O'Sullivan and Liam Donovan were both hardworking, the same age, bitter, and seemingly indestructable men, possessed by Ireland, by her troubles and

[34]

dreams, they were quite different from one another.

Liam was as fair as Brendan was dark. Liam had patience. Brendan had none. Liam could sing. Brendan could not. Liam had taught himself to read and to write. Brendan could do neither. Liam's earlier wanderings had given him a rudimentary education and a sense of worldliness. Brendan was a simple farmer who had never left the Ballingarry meadows where he was born. And as Liam's yearning for the open road quickly diminished after he met and married Kathleen O'Sullivan, Brendan's thirst for adventure grew. Soon, Brendan's soaring dream would turn into reality, although not in the way he had expected.

Some months later, Kathleen gave birth to her first squalling baby—a boy, Sean. And the destinies of Brendan O'Sullivan, the baby's uncle, were sealed.

"He needs milk, Liam," Kathleen pleaded. "I cannot nurse the baby. Sean needs milk."

"Don't worry, my darling, don't worry. I'll get him some. I'll buy some."

"With what?" Brendan asked. "We have no money. The Finnegan place lies fallow, they are gone, their two cows are gone. The nearest cows are up at the manor house."

"Then I'll go up there and ask the landlord."

"He'll not give it to you, Liam."

"I can ask."

"You're a fool. But I can get it for you. I've been visiting Annie Malone up there. She'll get it for me."

"But I am Sean's father, Brendan, not you. It's for me to go."

"Then go!"

Liam walked out into the cool night. Brendan followed him.

"And what if they turn you away, Liam?" Brendan asked him.

"Then I'll steal it!"

"No, Liam. They'll hang you if they catch you. You are needed here. The baby needs you. Kathleen needs you. You'll be no good to them dead. I am going."

With that, Brendan slammed his huge fist into Liam's jaw. Liam went sprawling on his back. The punch was not hard enough to knock Liam senseless. Liam got up and dropped Brendan to his knees with a hammering uppercut. Brendan, too stunned to move, shook his head as he watched Liam run across the field. He got up and ran after him. Brendan caught Liam part way up a small hill and knocked him flat again. As Liam rolled down the hill, Brendan ran toward the manor house. But Liam caught up with him. The two of them wrestled each other to the ground and rolled back down the hill, punching and twisting their way back to where they had started.

"If anyone steals around here," Brendan panted, "it'll be me. That's the least I can do for my nephew."

Again he slammed his huge fist into Liam's jaw. This time he did it while Liam was flat on his back and he was astride his middle. Liam went out like a light. Brendan picked him up and hauled him back into the hut. He put him on his straw bed next to Kathleen and the baby. Kathleen did not protest. The old man Seamus, having slept through the argument and battle, awoke.

"What happened?" he croaked.

"Nothing, Papa," said Kathleen. "Liam was very tired."

About an hour later, Brendan burst through the door of the hut. Cradled in his arms was a large tin of milk—about four gallons of it. Still trying to catch his breath after the flight from

[37]

the manor house down the hill to the hut with the weight of four gallons of milk in his arms, Brendan set the treasure down and wheezed, "A gift from me to baby Sean. Now you tell him that after I'm gone. Do you hear me Liam, Kathleen? You tell him that."

"In heaven's name, Brendan," Liam wanted to know, "why did you take so much? They are going to miss it and there'll be the devil to pay."

"Aye. They'll miss it all right. And what's more, they are going to know who took it, too."

"Where are you going, Brendan?" Kathleen asked.

"One thing at a time, my darlings. First of all someone up there—I don't know who—saw me squeezing the love out of Annie. Oh, that Annie Malone, Liam. I'll wager you never knew the likes of her in your travels. I'm going to miss her. Whoever it was who saw us sent a couple of bully boys after me and tossed me off the place. I let them. I waited a few minutes and went back. Annie, the good girl she is, was waiting. I told her what we needed. She showed me where the milk was. There were large tins and small ones. I took the biggest. And why not. You are going to need the lot."

"Brendan, they are going to be down here in the morning looking for you and the milk."

"Aye. I know it. That's why I must leave. Tonight."

"But where to?" Kathleen insisted.

"West to Limerick, first. After that, only the Good Lord knows."

"And what about Annie?"

"Don't you worry none about that dear lass. She'll squeeze the love out of the landlord's man and that'll be that. He'll forgive her her weaknesses."

Brendan put a few things in a small sack, kissed his sleeping father and turned to face his sister and Liam.

"Bury that tin in the soggy ground by the lake. They'll never find it. When they come looking for me, tell them I've gone to Kilkenny with the swag to sell it in the market."

The three of them, Kathleen, Liam, and Brendan, looked at each other. Not another word was spoken. Brendan ducked through the low door and disappeared into the night. Liam remembered another night, some twelve years before, when he had walked out of the Harrigan cottage and disappeared into the night.

7

The Donovan years slipped by so easily it was almost impossible to tell one from the other. More tenant-farmers, like their neighbors, the Finnegans, were evicted from their rented lands. Liam and Kathleen wondered when their turn would come. Brendan reached America and sent the first of several letters someone wrote for him—six years after he had left Ballingarry. He was in Boston.

October 29, 1839

Dear Kathleen and Liam,

I have come to Boston, Massachusetts in America. I have been to sea. Boston is a grand place. There is work for all.

There is money for every pocket. I work on the docks. I have not put a hoe into the ground since I left the old country. How is Papa? How is Sean? And you? If you can come we shall all be together. Please write to me. You can write to me at the Union Oyster House, Union Street, Boston, Massachusetts, America. I do not live there. Sometimes I work there when work is slow on the docks. It is a tavern.

God Bless you all.
Brendan

The money is for Sean.

Brendan had enclosed a five dollar bill. He had no idea how his family had grown and changed somewhat. Liam had set it all down on the worn inside covers of a battered New Testament —and this he began to do the day he married Kathleen:

June 1, 1832—Kathleen O'Sullivan is my wife

November 3, 1833—Sean Seamus Donovan is born

November 10, 1833—Brendan departed

March 17, 1835—Patrick Michael Donovan is born. Patrick for the Good Saint—Michael because Seamus says that is his second name. I do not believe it but it makes him happy

April 10, 1837—Maureen Nell Donovan is born. We name her for Kathleen's late mother

April 28, 1837—Seamus is dead—God rest his tired bones

February 1, 1840—A letter from Brendan in Boston, America

May 20, 1842—A letter from Brendan in Boston

January 11, 1845—A letter from Brendan in Boston

August 23, 1848—Mary Rose Donovan is born. Margaret Sheila Donovan is born

Liam would write in his Good Book again, soon. Meanwhile, these were the only events that he took care to note. Strangely, there was no hint of the terrible calamity that had befallen the family—indeed, had befallen all of Ireland. Misery, added to misery, compounded the centuries of unhappiness that ate at the soul of the ordinary Irish. But this calamity, this monstrosity, was the most unspeakable tragedy ever to have struck the glistening green land.

Famine! That was it. Famine! The starving time!

It fell upon the people during the late summer of 1845. An ax, so enormous, broad, and heavy that "only the devil himself could slam it into the heart of Erin," some said. The famine remained for five devastating years. At the root of it all was the staple food of the rural Irish, the potato—a sick and rotten potato, blighted by a fungus disease for which there was no cure. More than half the Irish needed their potatoes for more generations than they could remember. It was their only food. Now there were none.

"I am Ireland," Liam Donovan persisted. "My mother was the sweet earth of Kilfenora; my father a potato." But then he added, "And they have come back to murder me!" His children understood.

One and a half million Irish died. Another quarter of a million were too weak to bury them. A hundred thousand were thrown off their lands, unable to pay the rents; their homes leveled to the ground; their fields made into pasture lands. It was more profitable for the absent landowner to raise cattle and sell it abroad than it was for him to grow crops. Lucky the farmer who could still grow some food. He sold his food to pay his rent. The land was still his. But his family starved to death. A million more, penniless, landless, foodless, fled the green land of their past; fled the country they loved—rather than die.

Farewell to thee, Erin mavourneen.

The Donovans were a bit more fortunate than most. Not much. Just enough to keep them from the edge of absolute starvation. Several years before the famine struck, their landlord decided to cultivate fewer crops and increase his flock of sheep.

"There's more profit in it," the landlord's man told Liam as if more or less profit meant anything at all to the Donovans.

Gradually, the sheep took over the fallowed fields which were soon turned into grazing lands. The fields left to be cultivated grew smaller and smaller. The size of the crops were substantially reduced, accordingly. Liam, Kathleen, and the children continued to work the fields. And the harvest, however small, was still sent to market for sale. It never occurred to the landlord to turn over some of the produce to his tenants to stave off the specter of starvation that haunted them. Business was business.

Somehow, Liam, Sean and Patrick managed to store away some of that produce for their stomachs and for sale. The rent had to be paid, too. They never took that much to be noticeable. The landlord's man knew what they were doing but left them alone to nibble—but only to nibble. Yet, a nibble here and a nibble there—from their tiny garden of green vegetables—was just enough to keep them alive and hopeful. Their chickens gave them eggs from time to time. These, too, provided the Donovans with both additional nourishment and pennies for the rent.

[42]

Neither Liam nor Kathleen ever thought of using the five dollars that Brendan had sent from America. It was Sean's. Brendan said so. And it was Brendan who had risked his neck to get the milk for infant Sean—four gallons of it. And most of it was left to sour in the tin a week following the theft.

"The money belongs to Sean," Liam advised Kathleen. "When the lad is old enough, he will decide what he will do with it. We shall all get along without it. And may the Saints preserve us."

"It will take more than the Saints to preserve us," Kathleen replied.

Once the landlord's man caught Sean and Patrick rifling a basket of radishes. Taken by surprise, they froze as they were —bent over the radish basket. The overseer circled them, stalking his prey like a hungry, confident lion. Sean stared at the ground, his mind racing to find an escape. The rest of him remained unmoving, fixed to the spot like a marble statue.

Patrick, frightened but more guarded, warily eyed the overseer as he made his turns around them. Not once did he take his eyes from that menacing figure.

"And what do you suppose ought to be done with the likes of you two? Hanging? Hanging is too good for you—you thieving rascals."

With a hint of pity for the ragged, skinny, hollow-eyed boys and a small measure of scorn for the landlord's lessening interest in the dwindling crops, the man made up his mind.

"I'll let you go this time," he said gruffly. "But don't let me catch you at it again. If I do, I shall draw and quarter you like a piece of beef."

The peril over, Sean broke and ran. He disappeared without

so much as a backward glance, sure that his brother was right behind him. He was not.

The younger, more deliberate Patrick, emboldened by the small victory, defiantly walked away, all the while returning the steady gaze of the enemy—the landlord's man.

"We'll be back," Patrick promised himself as he slowly widened the distance between himself and the overseer, "only next time we'll be more careful."

It was not until he was halfway home and well out of sight of the overseer, that he too broke and ran.

8

"We are all that is left here, Liam."

Kathleen's soft voice startled her husband. These were the first words she had uttered in a week. Only Liam heard them, barely. Patrick and Sean had gone off in search of food scraps. Maureen was outside in the new spring rain pleading with the hens for more eggs. The baby twins, now eight months old, were asleep on a pile of straw.

Liam sighed with relief as he looked down at his half-starved wife. Kathleen's emaciated body had been wracked by a fever. The coal-black hair that framed her pale face exaggerated the translucent whiteness of her skin.

Liam touched her cheek. It was cool. The fever had passed. And Liam sang for the first time since the famine began:

'Tis pretty to be in Ballingarry,
'Tis pretty to be in Aghalee
'Tis prettier to be in bonny Rams Island
Sitting under an ivy tree.

Kathleen opened her blue eyes, once sparkling like the lakes of Ireland, now dull with the ache of hunger, the fever that cooled, and the dread of tomorrow.

"You sound like an angel, Liam." And then smiling she added, "And this wouldn't be heaven now, would it?"

"No, Kathy. We are where we are. Ballingarry."

"And we are all that is left here, Liam, aren't we?"

"Aye. The last."

"The Donahues? The O'Haras? The Mahoneys? The O'Connors?"

"Gone, Kathy. All gone."

"Then we must go, too."

"Soon, Kathy. Soon. When you have some strength."

"Now, Liam. Now. Before it is too late."

"And where shall we go? And how shall we get there with you unable to stand up?"

"We'll go to Dublin, Liam. To the city. It isn't far."

"It's far enough, Kathy. But suppose we did go to Dublin. What would we do there—the seven of us?"

"We'd find work to do, Liam. We'd hunger less. For God's sake, Liam, we shall waste away here—rot like the potato— and die, all of us."

"They are no better off in fair Dublin than we are here, Kathy. You know that. There is more sickness and death in that place than there is here. We are seven. They are better than one

[47]

hundred fifty thousand! And we are not going to rot away. Not you. Not me. Not the children. We shall do something. Now you sleep awhile and then we shall decide."

Kathleen closed her eyes and quickly fell asleep, exhausted from the brief discussion. Liam stepped outside in the rain. He hadn't been to Dublin since before he and Kathleen were married.

"That must have been seventeen or eighteen years ago, maybe more," he muttered to himself. "I did not like it then and from what I hear, I shall not like it now. That's no place for us to stay alive."

Images of present-day Dublin flooded Liam's mind. And what he saw were visions of eternal damnation—a fiery hell in which the poor screamed in everlasting torment and from which there was no escape. Liam was not altogether wrong.

Dublin, Ireland's largest and capital city, was in turmoil. Dublin was overwhelmed by the starving, dying refugees that poured into the already crowded, unpaved streets. There were not "better than one hundred fifty thousand" wanting souls in that place as Liam had told Kathleen. That may have been so twenty years before. Now there were at least a quarter of a million people threatening to tear the city apart.

There was no supply of fresh water in Dublin. There was no sewage system. There was no employment. There were few police—or none at all—to control the wandering, pleading, irritable mobs. Dublin reeked from the diseases that assaulted her, from the filth that rose from the streets, and from the unattended dead and dying that littered her alleys and lanes.

Dublin seemed beyond help. And Britain, however much she tried, was of little assistance. American ships brought corn to the tormented city. The British army set up great soup kettles to fill a few stomachs. And still the Irish died.

Mobs attacked the workhouses already too overcrowded with the poor. Worse still, the starving poor watched the cattle and grain come to the city and leave it for distant shores—sold for export. They tasted none of it.

Liam, soggy from the rain, watched as Maureen entered the cottage cradling one small chicken egg between her hands. "She is the picture of Kathleen," he mused.

Sean and Patrick approached him a few minutes later. Silently, and without expression, they held out their hands. They were empty. Not even a scrap.

Liam Donovan made up his mind. They would leave Ballingarry just as soon as Kathleen could stand—even if he had to carry her all the way to wherever their feet would take them.

"We'll go in the next day or two," he thought aloud. "We'll go west to Limerick, just like Brendan. And perhaps, like Brendan, we'll go to America."

Liam bent down and dug his hand into the mud at his feet. He picked up a fistful, opened his hand and watched as the ooze ran through his fingers and dripped back onto the ground.

"So be it," he murmured, "and let the good Lord protect us."

Part Three

Galway

There's a bower of roses by Bendemeer's stream,
    And the nightingale sings 'round it all the day long.
In the time of my childhood 'twas like a sweet dream,
    To sit by the roses and hear the bird's song;
That bow'r and its music I ne'er can forget,
    But oft when alone in the bloom of the year,
I think, "Is the nightingale singing there yet?
    Are the roses still bright by the calm Bendemeer?"
                    from *Bendemeer's Stream* by Thomas Moore

9

Liam Donovan opened his old and scarred Bible. He was alone in the cottage. The rest of the family waited outside to watch the orange sun rise above the eastern hills. Kathleen had recovered enough from her recent fever to begin the trek to deliverance. Sean and Patrick each held one of the twins. Maureen amused the babies.

The day promised to be bright and fair. A good spring day by any measure. Liam looked about him vacantly while thumbing the Book's pages. Finally, he wrote on the inside back cover:

April 21, 1849—Farewell to thee, Ballingarry

He stuffed the Bible into a small sack, flung the sack over his shoulder, looked around once more, and walked out to join his family.

"Patrick, my boy, go and fetch the wheelbarrow," Liam ordered. "We are not going to journey any distance burdened like dumb asses. How far do you think we'll get carrying the babies, the sacks and ourselves? We can hardly walk as it is. Here, let me have Maggie."

Patrick ran off and quickly returned with their large wheelbarrow. Liam threw his small bundle and several larger sacks into the bin. Kathleen and Maureen rearranged them, pushing and flattening the lumps for the benefit of the twins who were gently propped up against them. Kathleen covered the girls, who began to whimper, with a ragged and patched blanket to protect them against the early morning chill.

"Hush, now," she said. "That will be enough of that. Look at you two. Fairy queens, I'd say. Privileged. Be good, now."

The Donovans were ready for the unknown. And none of them were quite as hungry on this particular morning as they had been for months. Between the time when Liam decided they had to leave—five days ago—and this very moment, they had prepared themselves as best they could.

"Let us make certain," Liam warned, "that the lord of the manor knows nothing of our intention; and that none of us gives him any cause to wonder or suspect that we are about to leave this God-forsaken place. He will demand rent and tax which we will not pay. He will then evict us—drive us out like vermin. We will have none of that. We shall leave of our own free will—as free people. And when we depart, I want for us to look back and see this cottage still standing, not tumbled. We have suffered here but we have also loved here. And for that alone, for the love, we ought to have a decent memory—a lasting memory—of this place."

Everyone agreed enthusiastically. A great adventure was looming large, especially in the minds of Sean, Patrick, and Maureen. The whole idea of traveling somewhere, anywhere, of making a new home in another corner of the land or even beyond, buoyed their spirits.

Maureen somehow discovered a half dozen eggs she had previously missed in the rain. Now there were seven eggs including the one she had found the day before. These were boiled hard, wrapped in rags, and stowed away in a sack.

Patrick found renewed courage despite his frightening encounter with the landlord's man. He sneaked into the landlord's silo in the dead of night. Not once, but twice. The first time he helped himself to a sackful of grain. The second time he filched

[55]

a few healthy potatoes and cursed the landlord for having them.

Sean turned up with a bushel of greeneries to add to the family's own dwindling supply. He too risked his neck, remembering well the warning of the landlord's man to draw and quarter him—Patrick, too—"like a piece of beef." Yet, he made light of his haul.

"Where did you get those?" Liam demanded.

"Down the road." He would say no more.

Liam slaughtered their two hens. They were of no further use except to be eaten. Kathleen dressed and roasted them over the fire. The Donovans ate sparingly of one preferring to save most of the meat for the journey. Nonetheless, it was the first meat any of them had tasted in recent memory and it gave them some of the strength they would need. The partially eaten bird and its whole companion were tucked away in the same sack that held the grain, the potatoes, and the greens.

Now it was their morning. The orange sun had inched above the hills bent on its westward course. Liam grabbed the handles of the wheelbarrow, lifted and pushed. The wheels rolled. The journey began.

A few hundred yards beyond was a narrow dirt road that sloped northward with the dropping land. There the Donovans stopped at the last level point on the road and looked back at the cottage. The thatched roof was just beginning to catch the sunlight. From where they stood and stared the bright yellow highlights of the straw glistened like pure gold. Liam and Kathleen seemed unable to move as they watched the cottage come alive in the bursting light of the climbing sun. Sean, Patrick, and Maureen were less transfixed by the scene than their parents. The twins, comfortable in the wheelbarrow and oblivious to the whole thing, happily gurgled.

Patrick, growing more impatient by the minute, broke away from the silent group and ran down the road. Sean and Maureen chased after him. Finally, Liam grabbed the handles of the wheelbarrow once more, lifted and pushed.

"It's done, Kathy. We'd best be moving along."

The small thatched roof hut that had been the O'Sullivan and Donovan home for so many years slowly disappeared from view.

Kathleen, Liam, and the riding twins quickly caught up with the rest of their family at the bottom of the slope. From there the road arced northwest and uphill toward Thurles. The wheelbarrow with its cargo of provisions, possessions, and twins required little effort to move it downhill. In fact, it seemed weightless to Liam. But he knew better. This was not going to be a leisurely stroll.

Thurles, only twelve miles ahead of them, might just as well have been at the end of an endless road. The Donovans walked slowly, tired quickly, and rested a good deal. Liam and the boys took turns pushing the wheelbarrow. Sometimes Patrick and Sean each took a handle and pushed together. By sundown they had only gone six miles. They saw not a living soul. They met no one. That night they slept on the damp ground around a fire that Liam and his sons were able to make.

The next day, Sunday, was not very different—five miles more and Thurles was nowhere in sight.

Monday, the 23d, they were within a mile of Thurles according to an old farmer who pointed the way. But a driving rainstorm halted their trek and forced them to seek some shelter. Luckily, they found an empty and apparently vacated cottage.

[58]

It was much like the one they had left behind. There they spent the rest of the day and the entire night drying out and wondering whether or not the former tenants were on the road to somewhere, too.

The following morning, without concern for the misty drizzle that silently filled the air, they shoved and pulled their wheelbarrow through the mud, crossed the Suir River, and passed through Thurles.

Three days later they spent the night near Borrisoleigh before turning southward toward Newport and Limerick.

On Friday, May 4th, nineteen days and some fifty-five miles after leaving Ballingarry, the Donovans fell in with a long line of weary refugees like themselves and staggered into Limerick.

10

Limerick—**Luimneach** to the Irish—had been sitting on the banks of the Shannon River for a thousand years or more. But never in all those thousand years—during periods of conquest, turmoil, and indescribable violence—was Limerick subjected to the masses of sick and starving people who descended upon her during the great famine and fell dead on her streets.

Sixty miles west and downstream, between Loop and Kerry Heads, the great river freely ran out of Ireland. There the mountainous swells of the Atlantic rolled back and forth across her mouth, waiting with constant impatience to devour the Irish flow. Limerick was a river port to the world. And the hopeful came to Limerick to escape the doom that had settled over the green isle. Some did and fed their bloated bellies across the seas. Many did not.

It was late afternoon when the Donovans entered the city and melted into the noisy confusion. For the moment all they wanted was to escape from the jostling throng. Other than that they had no idea what to do next. Nearby a large crowd had gathered. More of an unruly mob than a gathering crowd— men, women, children, old people, and young people—elbowed and kicked each other mercilessly in an effort to get closer to whatever it was they were pressing toward.

The Donovans kept a respectful distance as they hung back and gaped at the incredible scene. Every so often someone would crumple or fall. If they were lucky, a good samaritan would drag them free of the tumult. If not, they would be trampled beyond recognition.

Suddenly, as if on a prearranged signal, the clamor stopped. The mob broke up and began to drift away. Remaining behind were a number of soldiers gently dispersing those who insisted on lingering. They had formed a ring around a donkey cart that held a large iron kettle. But now the kettle was empty, the hungry mob gone, and the soldiers were preparing to drive off.

"A gift from her majesty," remarked an old crone who had sidled up to the still gaping Donovans. "Hot corn soup in the merry month of May."

"Corn soup?"

"Aye, hot corn soup for the needy. America provided the corn. Ireland provided the boiling water. And Victoria sent the cooks. Where are you from?" the old woman asked in the same breath.

[60]

"Ballingarry."

"And where might you be going with those young ones?"

"We don't know," Kathleen answered. "Perhaps America."

"And where will you be staying the night here?"

"We are lost, grandma," said Liam. "Can you help us?"

"Do you have any money?"

"No," Liam replied, glancing at Sean as if to say, "not a word about that five dollars Uncle Brendan sent you."

"What do you have in those sacks?"

"Some personals. A little grain. That is all."

"Grain? Grain did you say? Here, let me have a look."

The old woman untwisted the nearly empty sack, jabbed her arm inside, and ran her fingers through the grain.

"Aye. That's grain all right. Share and share alike I always say. We'll share the grain and we'll share my palace. How does that suit you?"

"Fine!"

"Good! You'll give a lonely old thing like me some comfort. You can call me Maggy. Everybody does. Maggy Flynn. Born and bred I was in this lovely city of plenty. Never been anywhere else. Don't want to go anywhere else. Don't expect to go anywhere else—except to heaven, that is, if the devil himself don't claim my poor soul first. What did they call you back in Ballingarry?"

"Donovan."

"Donovan? Don't know any Donovans. Where did you find the grain? Is there more to be had?"

Maggy Flynn continued the steady chatter as she flew down the twisting, foul-smelling alleys, elbowing countless living skeletons out of her way—emaciated, hunger-wracked unfor-

[61]

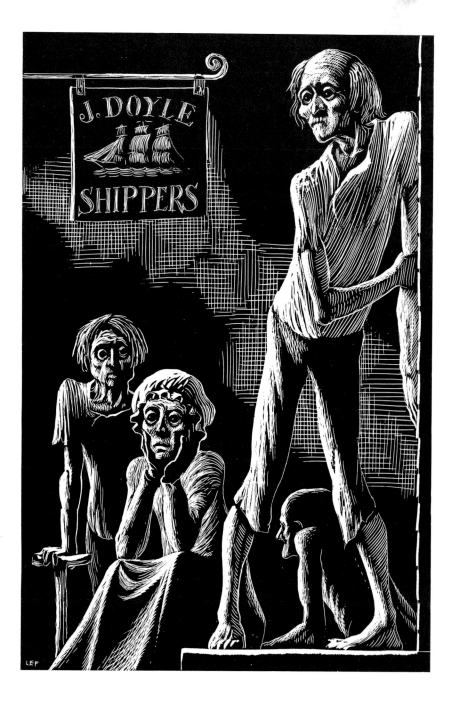

tunates with swollen stomachs and popping eyes, too weak to resist or step aside. The Donovans followed close behind, too stunned by the haunting scene to answer Maggy's questions. If Liam indeed did hear her, he remained silent, especially on the subject of grain. He preferred to let the old woman think there was more to be had. Perhaps, in this way, by keeping her guessing, they might be able to stay under her roof for more than one night. She might even find work for them. Finally, Maggy led the exhausted Donovans down a dismal alley and pointed to a miserable hovel at the far end.

"My palace," she announced.

A few seconds later they were inside the two-room shack, wheelbarrow and all. Maggy Flynn took the sack of grain and disappeared down a flight of steps.

"I don't think that old woman is going to let us live here forever," Liam told his family. "Not that we have a mind to. When the grain goes—and that will be in the next day or two—she'll demand more or something else. If we cannot satisfy her, she'll turn us out and take on other promising strangers. She is the landlord. We are the tenants. Soon more rent will be due. It is the make-up of the world."

"What will we do, Liam?" Kathy pleaded.

"Tomorrow morning, while you watch over the babies, Kathy, the rest of us will look for food, for work, for anything. And, if we cannot improve our situation, we'll move on. Warm weather is upon us. I'd rather sleep in an open field than this sickening place. However, it will do for now."

Not only did Maggy Flynn's "palace" do for that night, it "did" for weeks after. The Donovans, uncertain, afraid, and unable to come to grips with their predicament, seemed to stag-

[63]

nate at the end of the dead-end alley where Maggy Flynn had brought them. There was no work in Limerick for anyone, let alone the Donovans. From time to time Liam and the children watched the boats in the river. Every so often a large packet would fill up with those who had the price and drift downstream on its way to America.

Somehow or other, Maggy was able to add to the grain supply and provide enough nourishment for all of them—enough, anyway, to keep some flesh on their thinning bodies. No one asked her where she got the corn and vegetables. They were only too happy to eat it. By the end of the week, however, the grain ran out and as Liam had foretold, Maggy Flynn became less friendly. She demanded rent.

"Grain or coin," she told them.

Liam mumbled some promises. Eviction from their present squalor and absolute starvation loomed in their future. It would be their end. The Donovans were at their crossroads.

"You can still sing, Liam," Kathleen told him.

"I don't know. Who wants to hear an old minstrel?"

"You can try. You must. It is our only hope."

Liam and the children took to the streets. Wherever there was a likely gathering, Liam sang. In the beginning people listened and praised his soaring, rusty voice. But they gave nothing to Sean, Patrick, and Maureen who passed among them. But soon Liam's voice improved and so did the crowds. Little by little coins began dropping into the caps.

The Donovans paid their rent and saved the rest. Maggy Flynn became friendlier. They all ate a bit better. Liam's voice continued to improve. Toward the end of the month the Donovans made up their minds. They would go to America. They would leave Limerick and go to Galway where there were more opportunities to book passage.

Hope had returned to the Donovans. Liam wrote a letter to Brendan that they were on their way to Galway where they would seek a ship for America. The next day, May 29th, after having said their good-byes to Maggy Flynn, they pushed their wheelbarrow out of the dark alley and headed north for Galway.

11

For several days the Donovans followed the east bank of the Shannon River. The sun was warm and bright, the weather balmy. Five days later they reached Killaloe and crossed the river to the west side.

Tulla lay twelve miles directly ahead of them and they pushed on. About midway between Killaloe and Tulla, Sean and Patrick accidentally slammed the wheelbarrow into a large boulder, snapping off the wheel. There was little they could do to fix it.

At first Liam thought that he would send the boys back to Killaloe to find another. They could even buy one with the little savings they managed to collect in Limerick. But he changed his mind.

"We'll not go backward for any cause," he said. "We'll find something suitable in Tulla."

Liam picked up the twins. The boys picked up the bundles. Two days later they stumbled into Tulla. There Patrick found a derelict wheelbarrow. They did not even have to buy one. It

was larger than the one they left behind and a good deal heavier.

"I don't think we're going to get very far pushing this," Liam told everyone. "We are going to have to find some better means. Ennis lies to our west and that is where we shall head to lighten this burden."

Liam would have preferred to travel directly north. Now they were going west to Ennis, a place they could have traveled to directly from Limerick. All they did was circle around in a waste of time and energy.

In any event, they shoved the heavier wheelbarrow with its passengers and cargo ten hot miles into Ennis. There they stayed a week. It was too hot to travel anywhere. And there they rid themselves of the wheelbarrow.

Fortunately, Liam was able to put his voice to good use again. He sang the whole week long and managed to add a few more pennies to the family savings.

By the end of the week Liam had decided it was time to move on. But without a wheelbarrow or some other conveyance he was at a loss to figure out how to move his family with the least amount of difficulty.

"Perhaps I can buy something cheaply. We have a few pennies for that."

"We can't spend any money now, Liam," Kathleen responded. "There must be a better way."

"Patrick and I will look around," Sean offered. "Maybe we can find something for us. We'll be back soon enough."

An hour later, the boys came down the dusty road driving a small cart hitched to a donkey.

"Where in heaven's name did you get that?" Liam demanded.

"A miracle at last," Kathleen exclaimed.

"I bought it," Sean said proudly, "with Uncle Brendan's money."

"You should not have done that, Sean."

"Why not? I should have done it back in Thurles and we would have been in America by now. Besides I haven't spent our last coin. If I had that would have been different."

"Don't be harsh with them, Liam," Kathleen sighed. "It's for the best and you know it."

"Aye. And it'll be a pleasure to ride."

At sunrise of the following day, the Donovans squeezed themselves into the cart and drove off in the direction of Corrofin, some eight to ten miles away. They stayed overnight just outside the town and then continued on their way past Kilfenora. But Liam suddenly stopped the cart and turned it around.

"I want to see it once more," he said quietly.

And so the Donovans doubled back to Kilfenora, where Liam was born and abandoned by his unknown parents. The Harrigans were gone. The house was gone. There seemed to be no reminders. Liam walked around by himself for a short time, kicked the dirt, and climbed back into the donkey cart. The wheels rolled toward Ballyvaughan and Galway Bay.

The village of Ballyvaughan lay on the southern rim of Galway Bay about ten miles north of Kilfenora. Galway itself was across the bay directly north of Ballyvaughan and just over the horizon. The Donovans were unsure as to the best approach to Galway. They had a choice. They could either pay a fisherman to take them across the bay in his boat and thus enter Galway by a watery route. Or, they could take the long way around

[69]

by circling the eastern edge of the bay and enter the city by a land route. Liam and the boys wanted to find a fisherman to take them across.

"We have already taken too many long roads," they argued. "Besides, we want a taste of the sea and a breath of freedom in our lungs. We want to know what it will be like when we cross the ocean."

"You'll be getting a taste of the sea soon enough," Kathleen retorted. "We don't have to practice, you know."

Kathleen won. They circled the bay and passed through Kinvara and Oranmore.

Outside of Oranmore—not more than five miles from Galway—the road was choked with people bent with years of poverty and bound, like the Donovans, for the ships that would take them far away from their despair. Caught in the middle of this advancing army, the Donovans inched along. At times they hardly moved.

Finally, on Saturday, June 30th—seventy days and 135 miles from Ballingarry—a much relieved family drove their cart into Galway. As they entered the city they seemed to rise out of the dust of the road like a triumphant Roman chariot escorted by a weary, battle-tested legion.

12

Galway, or **Gaillimh,** was smaller than Limerick. But the scene was much the same. There were too many people, too much noise, filthy streets, and not enough water. Disease, hunger, and unemployment stalked every corner of the place. The only noticeable difference between Galway and Limerick was the ships in the harbor. Galway's harbor was alive with ocean-going sailing ships. In Limerick there were too few. This, at least, was the impression the Donovans got as they watched the crushing crowds push toward a half dozen gangplanks—the bridges to freedom and safety. Two of the ships cast off that very afternoon, their decks jammed with the sons and daughters of Erin. There were no excited good-byes, no happy waving—neither from those sailing away nor from those left behind. Only weeping. And when the ship disappeared from sight, some of the milling crowd remained to stare at the empty bay. The rest, clutching different passage tickets, joined the shoving crowd boarding the next vessel.

"Tomorrow," Liam said, "we'll find out about going to America. Now we must find somewhere to stay. We have only several days of food remaining—if we are careful—and we'll have to do something about that, too."

The Donovans slept in an open field that night hemmed in by a thousand more like them. The next day Liam and the boys drove the cart into the center of the city. Maureen stayed behind with her mother and sisters. The crowds were everywhere. Bony faces blankly stared up at them as they moved along. Liam had forgotten that today was Sunday. The shipping offices

were closed. There were no ships in the harbor either. They had all left. Only the several churches were open.

If Liam had any ideas about going to church, he soon gave them up. The churches were packed beyond belief, and it was impossible to get within a hundred yards of any one of them.

"We'll come back tomorrow," he murmured with a tinge of disappointment.

Liam and his sons returned to their camping ground where Kathleen, Maureen, and the twins were waiting.

It wasn't until late in the week that Liam was able to get inside a shipping office.

"How do we get to America?" he asked.

"How many are you?" the shipping clerk demanded.

"Seven."

"How much money do you have?"

"How much is the passage?"

"How much money do you have?" the clerk insisted. He seemed unwilling to give Liam any information.

Liam opened his bag of coins and spilled them out on the counter. The clerk began to sort them out.

"Tuppence, ha'penny, ha'penny, tuppence. You have nothing but pennies here. Not nearly enough. Next!"

"But, sir, how much is . . . ?"

"Do you have any American dollars?"

"No, sir. All I . . . ."

"Come back when you have more money. Next!"

Liam picked his way out of the office and confronted the first person he saw.

"Tell me, sir, do you know the cost of a passage ticket to America?"

"Well, that depends."

"On what?"

"On how many ships are available and ready to sail. And on how many people trying to get aboard."

"But what about the price?"

"Anywhere from twenty to fifty bob and maybe more. It's cheap as these things go. But when those shipping clerks take everything you've got—and that's what they want, everything —for a man who hasn't much, it's mighty expensive."

A shiver of panic ran through Liam's body. He was stunned by his poverty and the trap that now engulfed him and his family. What little money they had would have to be spent for food. And the price of food was high. He would have to find some way to earn enough for the passage.

Liam managed to jostle his way into two more shipping offices. He asked the same questions. He received the same answers. To make matters worse, there hadn't been a ship in the harbor for days.

"How do we stand, Liam?" Kathleen asked him when he and the boys returned from the shipping offices.

"Oh, we're a bit short, Kathy, not much. I'm going to have to sing again to fill our treasure chest."

Liam told no one the truth of their plight. That night as he lay on his back looking at the stars he thought of the five dollars Sean had spent on the donkey cart.

"We should have walked," he muttered over and over again.

For the next month, Liam Donovan sang on every Galway street corner. All he earned were enough pennies to keep them all from starving to death. And the open field was still their home. Their meager savings were gone. The donkey cart was gone. Liam had traded it away for a bag of hard Yankee corn.

Some ships came. Some ships went. But the Donovans remained behind, prisoners of their misfortune.

"I am Ireland," Liam cried out one night in his sleep. "My mother was the sweet dirt of Kilfenora. My father was a potato!"

Part Four

Grampus Rock

Farewell to thee, Erin mavourneen,
Thy valleys I'll tread never more;
This heart that now bleeds for thy sorrows,
Will waste on a far distant shore.

Thy green sods lie cold on my parents,
A cross marks the place of their rest,
The winds that moan sadly above them,
Will waft their poor child to the West.

13

July became August. Liam continued to sing and collect his pennies. The family kept away from the edge of starvation. Liam's voice was their suit of armor protecting them against the death-dealing horseman of hunger. Occasionally, not even Liam's golden voice was enough to gather an audience of a single misty-eyed soul. One such moment came during the first week of August. Across the street from where he sang to no one but his own daughter, Maureen, a fiery orator was busy denouncing England's Irish policies to a swelling throng.

"Oh, they want us to leave, they do. They want us to take the trouble with us. But it isn't easy I tell you! Where is there a greener land than this, our land, our Ireland? And where will you find a grander people than here, in our land, our Ireland?"

Liam and Maureen joined the crowd to hear what the firebrand, Donal O'Dell, was booming.

"Oh yes, they want us to leave to solve their problem. But let me tell you something my friends. It is Ireland the Lion wants. Ireland with Irish slaves. Never, I say! Never! Some of you will go. You must. But know that your flight from this oppression is the cruelest exile. For those of you who remain to suffer—and many will—be prepared. Slavery will be your handmaiden! Idleness awaits you! Starvation awaits you! Fever and death await you! The British Lion awaits you! And a fine dinner you'll make for the beast! Hear this, Victoria, you damned waterdog, Erinn go bragh! Ireland Forever!"

The crowd cheered and the old rallying hymn rose from their throats:

"Oh, Paddy dear, and did ye hear the news that's goin'
    round?
The shamrock is by law forbid to grow on Irish ground.
No more Saint Patrick's Day we'll keep, his colors can't be
    seen.
For there's a cruel law ag'in the Wearin' o' the Green."

Several British soldiers standing nearby made some menacing
moves toward Donal O'Dell. But they stopped. The chorus had
slowly drifted off and only one voice rising above the rest could
be heard—Liam Donovan's. For a moment or two it seemed as
if time were frozen for everyone within hearing distance of Liam
Donovan—including the soldiers. The power of Liam's tones
reached out and held them all like a vise.

When Liam finished, there was an awkward silence. No one
moved. But then the cheering started anew. Donal O'Dell
quieted the crowd which now numbered seventy or eighty.

"That, my friends," he screamed, "was the voice of Ireland.
Our Ireland. Let it ring out again!"

Liam began to sing again. Maureen mingled with the growing
throng. Coins jingled into her apron. Liam offered the money to
Donal O'Dell for his "mission," as Liam put it. O'Dell refused
to take any of it.

"I'm well taken care of, my friend. Look after yourself. You
have the voice of the angels and Ireland could use an angel or
two in this starving time."

O'Dell gave no further information about himself. Liam
didn't ask for any. O'Dell did make Liam an offer, however.

"With my tongue and your throat we can keep Irish hopes

alive. And that fair colleen of yours—your daughter—can collect what few coins there are. For sure, there'll be more pennies with us together than you alone."

Liam was delighted. Now there was a chance for the Donovans. For several weeks Donal O'Dell, Liam, Maureen, Patrick, and Sean crisscrossed Galway and the surrounding villages with what Kathleen called their "road play." After a while people gathered just to hear Liam sing the **Wearin' o' the Green.** They didn't much care how many times they heard him before, they went on asking for more. Liam and his new-found friend Donal O'Dell breathed some hope into the sagging populace.

"It was like that in the old days before we met and married, Kathleen," Liam sighed to his wife.

"What old days, Liam? The old days are still the old days. Nothing has changed," she replied.

"It has changed, Kathy," he cried out. "It has changed for us. I think we may have enough money for passage! What do you say to that?"

Kathleen Donovan did not say anything. It was too difficult an idea to grasp so quickly. True, they had talked a great deal about such a trip. They were planning on it. Yet, in Kathleen's heart it was still too much to hope for.

"Put me on the ship," she said, "and then I'll believe."

Liam would not be so easily brushed aside. "We are going to America. We are going to that place across the sea that God Himself had set aside for the poor, the hungry, the unwanted, the miserable, ordinary people of this world."

"You're making a speech like Donal O'Dell," Kathy cautioned. "It may not be as you imagine, Liam. It may not be the paradise you have in your head."

[83]

"Maybe not. But this I tell you. We are not going to live out our lives like beggers imprisoned in our own rightful land. We are not going to let our children grow to know nothing but fear and famine. America may be a savage place, for all we know. But at least they fought the devil and beat him. And we are going there!"

14

Liam spilled his large pile of coins onto the counter. Surrounded by Kathleen and the children, he watched as the shipping clerk slowly counted out the coins. Liam became so stiff and tense with apprehension that his huge fists, gripping the lip of the counter, turned a bloodless white.

"Do we have enough?" he asked.

"For how many and to where?" asked the clerk.

"Seven for America. Five are children."

"Not enough!"

"Not enough!" Liam bellowed.

He reached across the counter, grabbed the clerk, lifted him off the floor, and jerked him to within an inch of his red-angry face.

"If I do not have enough money for seven," Liam softly crooned, "then how many tickets can I buy? And if you tell me less than I want to hear, I'll break your greedy neck."

"You have enough for three," answered the terrified clerk.

"I'll have them now." Liam shoved the clerk back.

"You'll need travel documents."

"You write the tickets and I'll look after the papers. Write!"

"There are two ships in port bound for the United States of America," the clerk continued while rearranging his twisted jacket. "One for New York; one for Boston. Which will it be?"

"Boston. We've got a relative there."

"That will be the **St. John.** She sails day after next. That will be Thursday, September 2d. We'll post the time tomorrow. Now, who will be using the tickets?"

Liam did not hesitate. "Sean Donovan, Patrick Donovan, Maureen Donovan."

"My God, Liam," Kathleen cried, "what are you doing?"

"Hush, now, Kathy. Let us finish with this business. It's for the best."

"The best! The best of what? You are separating us! You are sending our lambs to the slaughter! What will become of them? And us? They in one world. We in another. An ocean in between."

"What will you have them do, Kathy? Rot and beg? Beg and rot? They are going first. They will find Brendan. In a month or two we shall have enough money again to follow them. Now stop your weeping. It is done and I am going to find Donal O'Dell. He'll know what we have to do about the travel papers."

But Kathleen Donovan would not be consoled. "If we cannot all go together," she sobbed, "then we should all remain here until we can."

"If all of us cannot go at once," Liam responded, "then some of us will go now. The rest of us will follow later. Sean, Patrick, and Maureen first. You, Mary, Margaret, and I next. That is the way it must be. We take the opportunity when it comes. And it

[85]

has come. Summer will soon be over. The children will not starve in America. And we shall have fewer mouths to worry about here. They'll be all right. We'll be all right. Temporarily, anyway."

The seven Donovans left the ticket office with three tickets. Kathleen continued to weep but Liam prevailed. Maureen held on to her mother, numbed by the quick turn their lives had taken, her spirit wavering, and too hungry to protest. Sean and Patrick understood the logic of their father's difficult decision and seemed to grow taller with the burden of their responsibility and the adventure that awaited them. Mary and Margaret—the twins—were altogether too young to understand. Before the year was over, they too would go to America with their mother and father. They would remember none of this; not Galway, not Ireland, not Sean and Maureen—not even their own voyage.

15

The brig **St. John,** tied fast to the wharf, gently lurched and creaked as the bay waters rose and fell beneath her. She wasn't much as ships go—especially passenger-toting, ocean-going wooden sailing vessels of the mid-nineteenth century. But then again, the **St. John** was never meant to carry people across the Atlantic Ocean. She was a square-rigged, two-masted freighter of some three hundred tons, built as a coastal trader.

The one hundred foot **St. John** had not been in the passenger business very long—a little more than a year. Her Irish owners were induced by attractive British government offers to try the North Atlantic run. Seaworthy vessels of all types were needed to export the starving Irish and lessen the burden of feeding so many. At the same time, the returning ships could bring back foodstuffs to nourish those who remained behind and managed to stay alive.

A large crowd began assembling on the wharf at dawn. The **St. John,** her sails reefed, creaked in the half light and waited for her human cargo. She would be ready to cast off at noon on the outgoing tide. A slight northeast wind and drizzle fell on the milling crowd at mid-morning, about the time the Donovans walked onto the wharf. The wind churned the water somewhat. White caps appeared and disappeared against the gray-green water of Galway Bay. The **St. John** strained at her ties, pulling them taut, in a seemingly impatient effort to catch the wind and sail away.

Some of the passengers were already aboard. The Donovans stared at the ship and watched others go up the gangplank— some with bundles, some with nothing at all—and step down on the wet deck. The Donovans surveyed the damp scene in silence. Sean, Patrick, and Maureen hung back. Their moment had come and they would soon climb the gangplank. They seemed unhurried.

Finally, Liam spoke. "It is time," he said quietly. "You must go. Remember, now, we all agreed last night that there will be no good-byes, no farewells. Our separation is temporary. It is a time for rejoicing, not weeping. We are all going to a better life. You Sean, and you Patrick, and you Maureen must look to the future—our future, all of us—and be strong. When you reach Boston, you will seek out your uncle, Brendan O'Sullivan and

you will tell him that we, your mother, the twins, and I, will join you all before the year is out. Go aboard now. And may the Good Lord look after you."

Kathleen swayed slightly but otherwise showed none of the stress and ache that had continued to clutch her since Liam had purchased the three tickets. Now that the decision had been made to send the three oldest children to America first—and that event was upon them—she had no intention of weakening the outlook of her children. She intended to show the same courage both she and Liam expected of them. Kathleen Donovan allowed herself to kiss her children. That was all. Sean, Patrick, and Maureen went aboard the **St. John.** Kathleen and Liam, with the twins in their arms, turned around and walked off. Both decided last night not to watch the vessel cast off and sail down the bay. It was better for all concerned to break off at the foot of the gangplank and not linger. That was the way Kathleen Donovan wanted it. And that was the way it was.

At noon, before a quiet and wet crowd, the green flag of old Ireland, emblazoned with a gold harp, broke out from the top foremast of the **St. John.** No one cheered. A few minutes later, the **St. John** let go her tethering lines and was towed out into the bay. There she remained for an hour while the crew made further preparations for the voyage ahead. Finally, the anchor was hoisted and the **St. John** moved down the bay, carrying some two hundred passengers to a promising land—America.

Not a single man, woman, or child was below as the **St. John** glided past their last sight of Ireland. Most of the passengers crowded the forward rails. At night they would be packed into the forward hole like the proverbial sardine. Some of the passengers—perhaps fifty in all—were assigned a small hold just aft of the main mast. They jammed the rails at midships. Sean, Patrick, and Maureen were settled in the forward part of the ship.

Now, they were as far forward as safety would allow, watching as the **St. John** turned south southwest and rounded Black Head to enter South Sound. By the following day, they had passed through the sound and were well clear of the Aran Islands. Hags Head had passed from view sometime during the previous night, and so had Ireland.

16

For four sunny weeks, the **St. John** rolled on the heaving Atlantic. The ship ran well, before a brisk wind that came out of the northeast and faithfully pushed them toward Boston, Massachusetts.

Yet, life aboard the **St. John** was primitive and dreary. There were enough barrels of fresh water to sustain them without rain for seven weeks. There were enough staple provisions on board provided by the owners and by the passengers themselves for about five weeks of minimum nourishment. If everyone was careful, they could stretch their meager supply of vegetables, grain, and American corn another ten days. Most of this found its way into soups of one kind or another which the passengers cooked themselves in the iron kettles positioned on deck near the entrance of the forward hold.

During the first week of the voyage, seasickness raged among the passengers. They ate little. Luckily, this was the only sickness at sea. By the end of that first week, everyone was up and around with nothing to do but watch the tireless ocean or find a windless place on deck to nap. The hold itself—the living quarter—was so dark, damp, and foul that no one went down there unless it was absolutely necessary. A few of the more hardy passengers never went down below, preferring to tie themselves to the deck at night and sleep under the stars.

There was much talk among the travelers about the future—about America—about what it would be like and what they hoped to find there. Rarely did the talk turn back to Ireland—not that every poor soul on that ship did not think of Ireland constantly. They did. But to talk of Ireland, the land they had just given up, would only bring to life unbearable memories. Whenever the monotony became too depressing—which was often enough—they would sing the lilting tunes that generations of Irish had sung before them and would continue to sing after them. That was their only show of sentiment. And when the singing would run its course, someone would always turn away to weep in private.

Sean and Maureen Donovan always joined the songfests. They felt closer to home and family that way. Ireland was still home to them however far behind the old country now lay. Sometimes, Maureen, in her dreamy longing, shut out every voice but Sean's imagining it to be the sound of her father. Not that Sean inherited Liam's musical gifts. Far from it. And Patrick often reminded his older brother of that fact.

"You do the heavy work, Sean. Let Papa talk to the angels."

"Don't mind what Patrick says," Maureen would urge. "You sound more and more like Papa, Sean. What does he know about such things anyway. Patrick has a clumsy ear."

Patrick never once sang aboard the ship. He could always be found at the rail staring at the endless sea. Day after day passed and always the scene was the same—cheerful blue skies, mountainous blue waves. Nothing else. It seemed to him that all they had done was to leave Ireland and their family to lurch around on a watery limbo without going anywhere, without arriving anyplace.

He thought some about Ireland but without any sense of loss. He was happy to be gone from that country; happy to leave the misery behind. He thought more about his parents and the twins. He missed them. But it was only a temporary separation. Soon they would all be together again. But Patrick thought mostly about the new world that awaited them. He thought about America with wonder and growing impatience.

When the captain announced one morning after three weeks at sea that they had sailed more than halfway across the Atlantic Ocean—dead on course—he refused to believe him at first. There was still that feeling of going nowhere; of only having come from somewhere; of being trapped by the deep water that surrounded them. But the excitement quietly grew within him and he began to watch the western horizon.

"Keep looking, boy," a passing deckhand called out. "She's over that edge, over there, just as sure as the sun rises and sets."

"America?" Patrick knew what he meant. But he asked just to be sure.

"America, boy. America."

While Sean and Maureen sang the songs of their native land on this floating piece of Erin—the ship **St. John**—and while others talked about what America would be like, young Patrick

Michael Donovan gripped the rail, kept his eyes glued to the horizon ahead, and waited for America to rise from the edge of the western sea bathed in a golden glow of heavenly light.

Near the end of the month the scene began to change. The ship turned directly west. The wind was still there pushing them, but the air turned warmer, damper. The sea became bluer, flatter. The **St. John** no longer bucked and rolled. Instead she sliced through the calm water with seeming speed, leaving a hissing white wake after her. She had entered the Gulf Stream about five or six hundred miles southeast of Nova Scotia. Now the wind changed direction and came up from the southwest, driving the **St. John** slightly north and off course.

A day or so later the **St. John** began to leave the Gulf Stream. Again the scene changed. A hard rain drove everyone below. The water was blue-gray, choppy, and white-capped. Having been blown slightly off course and too far north to suit him, the captain brought the **St. John** about in a great sweeping arc, took advantage of a whipping northeast wind, and headed straight for Boston. No one had sighted landfall as yet, but it was there, within reach. Everyone knew it. Gulls were now flying in their wake, diving at the pitiful garbage. Here and there a branch of a tree, some seaweed, a piece of food floated by.

The ship shivered, rose and fell, bucked and reared as the velocity of the wind increased. The rain came on stronger. The sea began to grow and swell. It slashed across the **St. John's** bow and flooded her holds. The skies darkened only to be lit again by sheets of lightning. The gulls were gone. The furious sea smashed at the ship and the ship fought back. The immigrants below huddled in masses, cowed by the struggle outside.

[93]

The captain had no idea where they were. It was impossible to take a bearing. At night the skies were black. There were no stars, no moon, no lights except the few that burned aboard the **St. John**—her bow, riding, and transom lanterns plus one in the crow's nest. The ship was virtually blind and being tossed about in an abyssal darkness by powers it could neither control nor understand. During the day the ship was just as blind. She seemed to be engulfed in a pocket of light that had no particular source. And from somewhere outside the pocket the ocean came at her with savage force. Rain beat her decks without let up. Thick, waterlogged clouds blotted out the sky.

The captain ordered the anchor dropped. "We'll ride it out here," he decided.

In the small midship hold that sheltered some of the immigrants, young Father Kevin P. Walsh—an immigrant himself —was comforting the terrified group. Most of them were so busy fingering their rosary beads, reciting and counting their prayers that they paid little attention to him. They could barely hear him above the storm, anyway. All during the Atlantic crossing, Father Walsh moved among the voyagers intent on his unassigned mission—cheering the immigrants, singing and joking with them, listening to their tales of woe and grief. And ever faithful to his calling, he listened to their confessions, gave communion, and celebrated the Mass.

But the young priest was not that deep in holy concentration that he did not notice a change in the ship's motion, fixed as she now was to an anchored station. He had been to sea from the time he was a boy to the time he left that life for religious study and the priesthood. He had sailed in brigs like the **St. John** as cabin boy and deck hand. He could sense every nuance in a ship's movement, storm or no storm. Since he had already made up his mind to go to the forward hold to soothe the others, he decided that now was a good time to find out what was going on outside.

Father Walsh pushed himself onto the slippery deck. Almost immediately he was picked up by the wind and slammed against the port gunnel where he hung on for dear life to keep from being swept overboard. Somehow in the darkness, after frantically groping for a more secure grip, he found a lifeline and slowly pulled himself forward. A crewman spotted him, reached him and grabbed him from behind.

"What in hell are you doing up here, Father?" he shouted.

"I've got to get to the forward passengers," he screamed back. "They need me. What's the situation?"

"We've got the anchor down and we're riding her out."

"Anything else I can tell them down there?"

"Aye. We've got a ship about two points off the starboard bow. There she is. You can see her now. Our top watch has reported several lights about three to five miles off the starboard beam," he bellowed. "Land lights. You'd better move on, Father."

The crewman stayed with Father Walsh until he reached the hatchway and disappeared down the ladder. At the bottom, Father Walsh could feel the **St. John** tug at her anchor cable.

"She's holding," he muttered to himself.

Quickly he surveyed the poorly lit hold jammed with frightened countrymen on their knees, praying. A sudden lurch of the ship knocked him back against the ladder and then hurled him sideways. He fell on top of Sean, Patrick, and Maureen Donovan. No one was hurt.

[96]

"I don't think the Lord knows I'm working for him," he joked. "If he did he would treat me with more care."

Sean helped him to his feet.

"I'm better off on my knees," he mused.

Those who heard his remarks laughed and some of the fright went out of them.

"Any news, Father?" Sean asked him.

Father Walsh told Sean and the others within earshot what he had found out. The word was passed around.

"Tomorrow is Sunday, my children," he added. "Tomorrow is the Lord's day. He will rest. Mark my word. Tomorrow it will be all over."

But the storm intensified during the night. The **St. John** groaned under the assault. Most of the immigrants dozed off unable to stay awake, exhausted by their fears and the constant pitching of the ship. Sean, Patrick, and Maureen fell into a deep sleep. Next to them lay Father Walsh, awake the whole night long, listening and waiting for whatever it was he could not be sure of.

Sometime during the early morning hours of Sunday, Father Walsh suddenly felt lighter, freer, drifting, and swaying forward. There seemed to be no power in the motion. Surely, none of the sails were broken out. The storm was still raging worse than before. Sea water was coming through some of the seams and showering the hold from above in fits and starts. For a moment he thought he heard screaming men above him. But the sound of the gale confused him. There was a peculiar bobbing to the ship's motion. She wasn't tugging and straining at the anchor cable.

"It's morning," he thought. And then it hit him!

"My God," he said half aloud, "she's slipped her cable! We're adrift! Mustn't panic! Got to get on top! See the situation!"

People were stirring. Sean, Patrick and Maureen awoke in time to see Father Walsh at the top of the ladder pounding the hatchway. The door was jammed. Something had fallen across it. They were all trapped below.

He turned around and faced the immigrants below him. A stricken expression masked his once cheerful appearance. He tried to say something. No words came. Possibilities raced through his mind as he stood frozen at the top of the ladder. The ship could sink, too weak to continue the battle. She had been taking on water for days and in this kind of weather what good were her pumps, if she had any to begin with.

The **St. John** could capsize, too tired to defend herself against the lateral pounding of the furious sea. She was already heeling dangerously and not righting fast enough. She could ram the vessel he had barely seen last night. She could run aground and be torn apart. None of them could escape alive from any of this.

It occurred to Father Walsh that they might by some miracle reach safety, but he discounted the reality of this so long as they were trapped and the storm continued unabated. Still he looked up and silently pleaded with the Almighty to work that miracle.

Again he looked down at the huddling humanity. Again he tried to speak. He moved his lips and stretched out one arm. Peering into the dim light, his eyes caught the uncomprehending look of the Donovan children who, like the rest of them, had come so far on empty stomachs and unbelievable courage. The **St. John** picked up speed and lunged forward with awesome power. Father Walsh crossed himself.

A shattering, unearthly roar split the storm. The helpless **St.**

John, driven by nature's madness, smashed headlong into Grampus Rock, one mile from Cohasset, Massachusetts—one mile from deliverance.

17

The mourners had begun to drift off when a chesty, black-haired, blue-eyed giant of a man jumped from a wagon. He was dusty and breathless.

"Am I too late?" he asked a tearful woman.

"Aye. The service was short and simple. Did you lose someone in the disaster?"

"I don't know," he answered, looking around at the slowly dispersing crowd. "I have some relatives coming over but I can't be sure that they were aboard this particular ship. I heard the news and came down here as fast as I could."

"Family name?"

"Donovan."

"Can't say that I recall that name. You might ask some of the others here."

"Donovan? Yes. I think there were several Donovans on board," someone added who had overheard the brief conversation. "But that's a fairly common name, you know. They may not be your relatives. Do you see that man over by the large wagon? That's Tim Murphy. He may be able to help you."

"Thank you."

The tall man strode over to the wagon. "Are you Tim

Murphy?"

"Yes. And who is asking?"

"My name is O'Sullivan. Brendan O'Sullivan. They told me you might be able to help me."

Tim stared at Brendan. "Perhaps I can. Perhaps I can't. Tell me Mr. O'Sullivan, are you from Boston?"

"Indeed, I am."

"Can you tell me exactly who it is you might be searching for?"

"The Donovans. Do you know anything about the Donovans? Were there any Donovans aboard that ship?"

"Easy now, Mr. O'Sullivan. I don't think you ought to get your hopes up. How many are they? What are their Christian names?"

"Well, Mr. Murphy, they did not write to me except once. That was last May. I haven't seen them for many years. When I left Ballingarry—that's where we are from, County Tipperary —there was Kathleen, my sister, Liam, her husband, Sean, their first born—there may be other children, I do not know—and Seamus, my father."

"I can tell you this much, Mr. O'Sullivan. There were Donovans aboard the **St. John.** Three. Young ones. We buried none of them here."

"Thank God for that much," Brendan remarked.

"I can take you to one of them. A boy. Alive and well."

"What of the other two?"

"That, Mr. O'Sullivan, you will have to find out from him— provided of course he proves to be a relative."

Brendan climbed into Tim Murphy's wagon. The two of them drove down to the beach where Patrick Michael Donovan still

[101]

sat. Abigail was there, too, several yards behind him, sitting on a log. She spotted the wagon coming toward her and got up to greet her husband. But the wagon stopped far short of where Patrick sat. He was unaware of the activity behind and to the left of him. He continued to watch the restless water.

"There he is, Mr. O'Sullivan." Abigail had reached the two men. "This is Mr. Brendan O'Sullivan, Abigail. Mrs. Murphy, Mr. O'Sullivan."

"How do you do, madame."

Abigail knew that Patrick Donovan's voyage was now over.

"I think, Mr. O'Sullivan, that it would be best if you spoke to the boy alone," Abigail said. Tim agreed. "We'll wait here."

Brendan climbed down from the wagon and walked toward his nephew.

Timothy and Abigail Murphy watched from a distance as th man and boy talked. Finally, Brendan and Patrick clutch each other and slowly walked back toward Tim and Abi

"Will you show us one more kindness, Mr. Murphy? you drive us up to my wagon? Patrick and I are going h